"When the whole universe seems a vast practical joke
it breeds a genial desperado philosophy."

Herman Melville

Wittgenstein's Lolita

The Iceman

BY WILLIAM GAY

© 2006 William Gay

ISBN 0-9765202-2-2

First Edition

Cover Illustration by William Gay

Book design by r.e.bright

Author photo by J.M. White

Published by:

WILD D🐾G PRESS

91 Vantrease Road

Brush Creek, TN 38547

CONTENTS

Wittgenstein's Lolita

Through a deep blue dusk that fell at the very end
of a season of ruin he came up past the landscape of
ruin itself. Looming palely out of a coming dark were
statuary, birdbaths, Madonnas, unarmed Venuses,
capering cherubim, shapeless shapes past all identify-
ing. The yard as it climbed toward the yellowlit house
at its summit looked like a dumping ground for sculp-
tors, the repository for misbegotten art that resulted
from clumsy hands, hangovers, dementia praecox. A
yard sale from the attic of a madhouse.

He climbed the high wooden steps to the porch and
knocked at the front door and waited. He turned and
looked back down the slope to where myriad concrete

figures regarded him like a community of ghosts out of the falling dark. Past the fence the woods were already lost to night and they looked like dull blue smoke.

Hey, a voice said. He turned to face a young woman regarding him from the doorway. She'd only opened the door part way and its edge bisected her face so that he could see half her face, one red braid and one green eye, beyond her the paneled interior of the room, a worktable, a greenlit computer screen. There was a gun cabinet and he studied the cased guns with a kind of focused interest.

Hey, Rideout said. I don't want to bother you. I just seemed to have misplaced a dog.

Her face was pale and smooth as one of the broken venuses he'd passed and some expression he couldn't name flickered across it and gone like a hairline crack appearing and vanishing.

Who are you?

My name's Rideout. We never met but I live back across that field, where you can see the light at night. I thought your husband might be at home. I hear him shooting over here sometimes and I thought he might have seen a dog back in the woods.

Actually this wasn't what Rideout thought at all: he'd been sitting in a lawn chair at the edge of the field wondering where the dog was when the shot came, a short exclamatory crack suddenly warped and elongated by the echoing woods and he thought, no, he knew: That son of a bitch shot my dog.

She'd stepped backward to permit Rideout entry to the room. The light was better here and he saw her face wasn't smooth and perfect after all. A fading bruise at the corner of her left eye marred it, cerise where it began and fading to the faintest of blue above her cheek bone and vanishing. As if, he thought, she'd been crying and wiped her eyes and smeared bluegreen tears.

He's not here, she said. But I guess I could ask a neighbor in and offer him a cup of coffee.

Maybe I shouldn't, he said, but he was already edging into the room.

It's all right, the coffee's already made. I was trying to write a poem. I drink coffee when I'm doing that, but there's plenty left.

If you were writing a poem I guess that must mean you're a poet.

Actually it just means I was trying to write a poem.

He sat awkwardly at the kitchen table. The windows had gone opaque with dusk, turned the room in on itself. He saw himself mirrored enigmatic and oblique, faintly sinister, an interloper in this cozy room of warmth and spicy smells. The glass reflected the woman behind him, turning from the counter, a cup of coffee in her hand.

What kind of dog is it? she asked.

Was it, Rideout thought.

Kind of a mixed-up dog, he said. Part pit bull and part bull dog. A gray dog pretty big in the chest and head. He's harmless though, good with kids.

I haven't seen your dog. Does it chase cows?

Does it what?

Chase cows. Those cows out in that field, they belong to Lynch or somebody. The man that owns that field and lives in town. He's talked to my husband about it, about looking out for dogs. There are wild dogs back in those woods. Maybe a pack of coyotes. They've killed a couple of calves and Lynch told Albert he'd pay him so much a dog if he'd kill the ones that were running cows.

He doesn't run cows, Rideout said, sipping his coffee, thinking he should be gone, wishing he'd never come here. He didn't see many people much anymore and he felt that such social graces as he'd possessed had fallen from him. Conversation was a burden of such weight that he could still pick it up but he couldn't carry it very far.

I'm such a fool, I never get any company and I don't know how to act. My name's Rebekah Faust.

She spelled Rebekah for him. He'd noticed that she kept glancing at the clock on the kitchen wall. She seemed nervous.

We ought to talk more, she said. I don't have anybody much to talk to and he's gone most of the time. He works the boats, but he's in this weekend and it's about time for him to get in. He may be drinking.

There were worlds implied here that Rideout didn't want to acknowledge, much less explore. The fading bruise was her own, none of his business. No more his business than the wedding picture that having set his cup aside and crossed the room he stopped momentarily to study. She looked happily unbruised, yet somehow tentative, smiling into the camera the smile you smile when you have flung the dice and are caught in the moment when they are still in motion and you are waiting to count the dots. The man she was clinging to was heavyset, goateed, but instead of tentative he looked satisfied and self-possessed. Judge us by this, the face said. We are happy and we've got our good clothes on and there's going to be a party and nothing bad has happened yet. There were, there are, there will be other moments, but judge us by this one.

He went out feeling oddly as if he'd stolen something, caught her eyes turned elsewhere and slipped
part of her life into a side pocket and made off with it.

Crossing the fence beyond the revenantial statuary
he could see carlights approaching down the long curving driveway and without knowing quite why he
increased his pace into the field toward his house. Still
the lights washed him before he was out of sight and he
was frozen in their glare like a deer in a spotlight. The
lights yawed away, vanished, a car door slammed.

Silence then a voice loud but suddenly muffled by
the closing of a door with only the quality of anger or
accusation retained and he wondered if there was
anything he could or ought to do but he went on like
a sneakthief who can only be comforted by distance
and darkness.

Like bad news she was sitting on the stone doorstep
awaiting him when he cut the truck engine in his front
yard. Red hair unbraided now and long down her back
and when he'd closed the truck door and approached he
could see where it held the crimps still and the crimps
caught the light like hammermarks in soft copper. She
had her hands shoved deep into the pockets of her
denim jacket and she was shivering from the cold.

You could have gone in.

Well. You weren't here. I didn't feel comfortable with that. I knocked but no one came to the door. I thought your wife might be here.

I don't have a wife, he said.

Oh. Have you ever been married?

My wife is dead.

Oh, I'm sorry. So you live alone?

He thought about the dog. I guess I do now, he said. It was so cold he could see his breath.

Come on in. Maybe it'll be warmer inside.

It was but not by much. He was using only the fireplace for heat that year and it had burned nearly out. He turned on the light and the room leapt at him: the paneling of old barn lumber, the room merciless in its clutter of magazines, tottering stacks of books. Had he known she was coming he would have neatened it. It had been a while since there'd been a woman here. He could have made herbal tea. Perhaps baked a cake. He crossed the room and with the poker raked up the coals in the fireplace, knelt and stacked kindling atop them, laid on wood. He wondered if he ought to put on a pot of coffee.

Has Albert been over here?

Albert who?

Albert. My husband.

I haven't seen anything of him. Why would he be?

God, she said. I'm glad of that. That would have been so embarrassing. He said he was coming over here, he was making all these wild threats. He's a little crazy sometimes. He's gone on the boats a lot of the time and he's always accusing me of going with men while he's gone. He saw you the other night and thought you were a lover fleeing with your pants in your hand. He can get a little rough sometimes.

Rideout decided against coffee. He doesn't need to be coming around here doing that, he said.

Doing what?

Getting rough on another man's property. That's trespassing. You can get in trouble like that.

He was born to trouble, she said. Trouble is what he does best. He seeks it out. You don't have to worry though. He's on the boats again, he won't be back for a couple of weeks.

I wasn't worried, Rideout said.

What I came about, you remember asking me about your dog? I can show you where he is.

Rideout turned from the fire. Where? He asked.

You might want to bring a shovel, she said.

They crossed a field fallow save for the winter stalks of weeds, brittle and fragile under their feet, the air going bluelooking and cold. A few dizzy flakes of snow whipped upward by the wind, the west just a dull metallic glow, a wan and fugitive light. Against it the grove of pines darkening, every color but black bled away.

They were nearing the woods, her leading, Rideout with the shovel slung across his shoulders like a deer rifle. A demarcation of barbed wire divided field from wood.

I saw the strangest thing here one day, she said, her voice taking on the quality of a storyteller commencing a tale, and in time to come Rideout would decide that everything that happened grew out of the stories they told each other. Everything they were to each other, everything they were not. Threads from one tale crept to another and bound them as inextricably as a particular sequencing of words binds teller to tale to listener.

I came by here late one day back in the fall, I'd just been walking on those old wagonroads or whatever they are. I was trying to write a poem and I couldn't think. Sometimes walking helps me to think. Anyway I came up that old road and there was a woman sitting on that wooden gate.

She pointed. This woman, I couldn't see her face real well, she was young, I could see that.

I spoke to her and she just looked at me like I wasn't there. I thought the hell with you then, if you want to be that way. She was wearing a red and black checked shirt, a hunting shirt, you know the flannel kind with the thermal lining? That's what she was wearing.

They'd reached the barbed wire fence, crossed, Rideout pushing down the top strand just so to aid her passage across it.

Here's the strange part. I went on toward the house. I wasn't going to look back, but then I did. She was gone. I mean gone like that, that quick. There was no woman there at all. Where did she go?

I don't know, Rideout said.

The memory of a road went curving palely into the wood. This way, she said. There'll be some cow bones or horse bones or something. They followed the faint road. Off in the indigo trees leaves drifted invisibly, rose and subsided with the wind.

Off in the winter huckleberry bushes lay the skeleton of a cow. Rideout studied the predator-scattered bones, the horned skull. Looking perhaps for rotted swatches of red and black flannel. Kicked a flat halfpint bottle out of the dead leaves, wanting a drink for the first time in a long time, wondering what freight of dreams or visions the bottle had carried.

Here, she said.

The dog lay on its left side in the leaves, stiff legs scissored as if it had died reaching for more distance than there was left in the world. It had been shot from an oblique angle and the bullet had slashed open the belly as neatly as a knife unstitching a seam and its ropy blue intestines were coiled over the leaves like unsprung parts. Its eyes were open and its teeth bared as if it would attack whatever hand had jerked it so suddenly into the darkness.

That dirty son of a bitch, Rideout said. That cocksucker. This dog never ran a cow in its life.

She didn't say anything. Her face looked white and pinched from the cold. Rideout raked the wet black leaves away with the blade of the shovel and began to dig a grave.

The Shaefers had it made when they lived here, Rideout said. He had the perfect job, in business for himself. Making money hand over fist. They had this great house, he had a wife and kids. Then one day it all blew up in his face like a landmine. This is a luckless place if there ever was one.

We bought it from the bank, Rebekah said. We got a good deal, they wanted to unload it.

Albert keeps saying he's going to haul all that junk to the dump but he hasn't done it yet.

I don't know but I'd keep this stuff, Rideout said. It gives the place atmosphere.

It's a lot of crap, she said. All those statues everywhere. It's like people watching you all the time and they never say anything.

They were sitting on her porch. Looking across the winter field, to woods austere and secret.

She'd been telling him about Albert. Albert who worked the barges and plied the river like a Kentucky boatman, riding them to New Orleans and Natchez for weeks at a time, reappearing with his sudden gifts of violence like souvenirs he'd picked up in these exotic ports of call. She clasped onehanded in her lap a Richard Hugo book she'd borrowed from Rideout, her other hand raised a glass of wine to her lips. Rideout sipped at an inch and a half of Grand Marnier in an old fashioned glass.

Had it made, Rideout said again. He made all this stuff, he had molds and he cast it out of concrete, all these saints and Jesuses and concrete deer. Sold it all over, he had contracts with department stores all over the south. No telling how many of those birdbaths he sold to Wal-Mart, he had four or five trucks delivering the stuff.

He had a fifteen year old boy named Dexter. One day everybody was gone but Dexter. For no reason at all Dexter drank four or five beers out of the refrigerator and decided to go for a ride in his mother's Mercedes. He came around a curve like a bat out of hell on the wrong side of the road and ran head on into a pickup truck carrying a woman coming back from picking up her two kids at school. Dexter died, the two kids in the truck died, the woman lost a leg and almost died.

You can imagine the lawsuits. Huge stacks of paperwork. Everything fell apart. The kid had no license, no insurance, no anything. Nothing but a sixpack and a Mercedes. Shaefer's wife took off with an anesthesiologist. Shaefer stayed and fought judgements and wrongful death lawsuits. He poured money down legal ratholes until it was gone and then one night he just eased away. Nobody had a hint where he went, he might be in Singapore or his bones might be laying out there in the woods where he blew himself away. Nobody knows. The house stayed empty a long time and then one day I heard shots. That night I walked over here.

It's too cold out here, she said. You want to come in a while?

I need to go.

Come in a few minutes. I want to tell you a story.

Inside she made tea and then sat on the couch sipping it from a thin porcelain cup, Rideout in an armchair with his cigarette and replenished cognac.

I really wish you wouldn't smoke in here, she said. Neither of us smokes and Alfred will smell it. He's always sniffing around for something to be suspicious about.

Rideout made ready to go. I need to be off anyway, my fire'll burn out.

Oh, go ahead and smoke, the hell with Alfred. But let me get you a saucer or something to ash in.

It's funny how things fall apart, she said when she was seated again. Take me and Alfred. We were childhood sweethearts and we were going to be together forever. The whole bit, grow old in rocking chairs and be buried side by side. Be reunited, roll around Heaven all day. I was going to be a poet, he was going to make it in the music business. He's still got a rock band he fools around with when he's sober enough. How do you get from there to here? Where's the point when it all changes?

She fell silent. Rideout watched her. They hadn't turned on a light and in the dim room with its dark paneling and just pale winter light at the windows she looked provisional and oddly transparent, as if the past she'd lost refused to give her up and was slowly repossessing her.

Let me tell you what Alfred did one time, she said. This was the damndest thing. It was a couple of years ago and we were living up in Williamson County. We were separated, we were always separating and getting back together. This time it was particularly awkward because we were both working at the same place. The Williamson County High School. I was teaching English and Albert was the maintenance man. I guess you'd say janitor. Except it got to the point where nobody knew where he was. People would need something done and then they couldn't find the maintenance man. His car was in his parking place, he was clocked in, but nobody knew where he was.

Then somebody kept noticing sand on the floor of the teacher's lounge. Every day, sand. Nobody could figure out where it came from. Finally one of the teachers got a ladder and climbed up and took out one of the ceiling panels. And what do you think they found.

Rideout felt a little drunk. He'd given up alcohol for a long time and he was mildly amazed at how easily he fell back into the way of things. I don't know, he said.

This was a dropped ceiling with a metal framework to hold the ceiling tile and above were the joists and rafters. Alfred had laid plywood on the joists to make a kind of floor. He'd carted all kinds of things up there. Sand, mortar mix, dirt, pieces of lumber. Tools. He'd built a farm up there, dirt hills, a creek with a little bridge across it.

But the strangest thing was that it was a replica of the place we lived when we first got married. It was an old farm house and he'd made a model of it that was complete to the last detail. The tin roof, the little stone chimney. At night we used to lie in bed and listen to the train go by and he'd even built a model railroad that ran back behind the hill. There was a tiny Alfred and a little me sitting down by the creek. It was spooky. I thought about him lying up there at night, wrapped up in his quilts, watching the house we used to live in, remembering the things we used to do. I wonder what he thought about?

Rideout didn't say anything. He thought they might be talking too much, loose lips sink ships, things with nowhere to go always wind up going somewhere anyway.

They came and got me, she said. The principal did, and made me go up and look. They thought I could explain it. Hell, I couldn't explain it. I wanted an explanation myself.

They fired Alfred, and I quit because they did. Then we got back together. What do you make of that?

It was cold in the room. Through the window the bleak fields looked colder yet and Rideout was dreading the halfmile walk to his house. But he decided to go there. He thought of the warm fireplace, a pot of hot coffee. Blues on the stereo. He thought about her question but he didn't have an answer for it. Try as he might he didn't know what he made of it. He thought how much simpler everything would be without the baggage you accumulate going through life. All the dog carcasses and dead wives and tiny houses that come back to haunt you. If you could just deepsix it all over the side and keep moving. If you could just slide through customs with nothing to declare.

It was very cold in the field. The world was all earth colors, umber and gray and ochre, a charcoal smudge of smoke from his chimney and the air was so cold everything viewed through it seemed vibratory, a world that would not hold still. The air in his nostrils felt like ice and smelled of cedar, sagegrass, crushed pine needles. Where am I going and why am I going there? he asked himself.

Down the hall one drunken night they fought like mad folk. Albert's fists coming like pistons, a right, a left, rising and falling like a knocker's hammer, slamming against her hands where she clasped her face, a jab to the ribs that filled her lungs with fire, her bouncing wall to wall and careening off doors and spinning down the hall clawing at doorknobs that wouldn't turn. She screamed at him, she flailed at him with a vacuum cleaner hose, a lamp that flared and died, a TV Guide. She slammed against a door that sprang open behind her and spilled her onto the carpet and she scrambled up already running but it was a room full of walls with nowhere to run.

Her head was full of light. Everything was a garish comic book with stars circling her head and cuckoos chirping and meaty blows that sounded like exclamatory sound effects, thud to the ribs and wham to the head and kapow when her head slammed the cedar chest and she went down to darkness.

You've got to get the hell away from him, Rideout said.

I know it.

Then why don't you do it?

Well. I had him locked up. He's in jail now.

For how long?

I don't know. Till somebody bonds him out. So far he hasn't found anybody. Then there'll be a trial, something, I don't know. I guess he'll go back to jail. I'm not dropping charges this time.

This time?

Usually he hits me where it doesn't show. This time he really freaked out. But by the time the cops came he'd apologized a dozen times, he was sitting there with his head in his hands.

God. The poor guy.

She didn't say anything.

Get an injunction to keep his ass away. Throw him out. It's your house too.

He makes good money. I'd be throwing myself out too. I can't make the mortgage payments until I find a job. I've just got to figure all this shit out. I'm leaving him when he gets out.

He was silent a time. Finally he said, You could stay here until you figure something out.

She gave him a rueful smile. He'd figure something out first, she said. He'd kill us both.

He thought maybe he wouldn't see her for a while. He'd finally gotten some peace in his life and somehow it didn't seem so peaceful anymore. He was working as a carpenter then and some days he'd just be home long enough for a shower and then he'd head out. He didn't want the phone to ring and he didn't want her to come walking across the field with a book in her hand and he didn't want to think about her at all.

He spent long hours sitting in the City Café slowly drinking draft Budweiser and listening to the incessant tale telling of the old drunks who haunted the bar like ghosts of their own youth, regaling each other with deer they had killed, snipes they had hunted, cows they'd tipped over, money they had made and pissed away, improbable women they had screwed. Rideout still and attentive and respectful as if he'd learn of life at the feet of these old sages.

There was a jukebox here and it was stocked with country records out of an older time and he'd sip his beer while dead steel guitar players plied their craft and Ernest Tubb sang across the void in his nasal Texas twang, Let's say goodbye like we said hello, in a friendly kind of way.

He slid his glass across the bar. Hickey, you ever know Albert Faust?

Used to. He used to hang out in here some. It's been a while though, I don't know where he's got off to.

Somebody said he was workin the boats. Why?

No reason, Rideout said. He bought that Shaefer place where they made statues and stuff.

The casting place.

Hickey overfilled the mug and whisked the foam away expertly with a ruler and set the beer before Rideout and took up a bill from the bar.

He was always one of these guys things never fall right for, Hickey said. Couldn't win with loaded dice, he could find a twenty dollar bill in the street and it would turn to counterfeit before he could make it to a store. A diamond would turn into a little bitty turd in his hands.

On the jukebox George Jones said, But I know it's true cause I was watching you, from the window up above.

Hickey laughed.

What?

I just remembered something he done one time. He was workin for the city, he was some kind of cop, constable or something. Wore a uniform and toted a pistol. He always wanted to tote a pistol. They had all this goin on about drugs in the schools and they was always lookin for dope in people's cars. Albert come up with this drug sniffin dog. I don't know where it come from, I guess the county paid for it. Albert might of got it off the internet. It'd been off to school, had a diploma and everything. A drug sniffin dog.

Albert took it up to the school parkin lot. He was goin car to car with it when it just started raisin holy hell tryin to get into this beige Lincoln. Albert called the number in and they run it. It was some English teacher named Odom. Albert got the lock jimmied some way and turned that dog loose and between the dog and Albert they just tore hell out of that Lincoln. Teetotally wrecked the upholstery, Albert tore the dash out of it. Come to find out all there was in the car was a Hardees sausage and biscuit under the seat. They fired Albert's ass. I don't know what they done with the dog.

Single file they came through the frozen woods, the earth hard as stone underfoot, their breath a smoking vapor that haloed their faces. Leaves clashed in a soft hush musical as wind chimes. The path wound through black charred looking trees. Startled birds rose with wild harsh cries before them, a cloud of blackbirds moved shapeless and ephemeral as smoke.

They had come to a clearing, a barren circle surrounded by lofty pines with trunks like the bones of a ruined cathedral. Rideout sat on a fallen log and pulled off his gloves and lit a cigarette. She stood watching him. Rebekah was bundled up in a woolen peacoat and a Navy watchcap. Her face was a motley of colors, saffron, cerise, a delicate blue, and it still looked oddly misshapen.

We could be sitting in front of your fireplace, she said. Is there something particular about this story that requires you to tell it in the middle of these woods?

I thought it might be easier out here, he said. I've never talked about it to anybody. Walking makes poetry easier for you, right? I come out here a lot, he said. Not as much as I used to but probably more than I should.

He toed the cigarette out beneath a boot. He looked up. She was watching him and she looked as if she were going to say something and then she didn't.

I used to love these woods, he said, feeling his way into the past. Then they changed, it's hard to explain in just what way, but they feel different. When I was married I lived there where I live now. I was a carpenter then too but I was working for someone else instead of myself. But there was a future coming up, I could see it. We were young and happy. Or I thought we were. Later I learned that it was just me that was happy.

Things changed, or she changed. She'd look at me and not see me. She got distant, it was like watching her walk across that field through the wrong end of a tele-scope, she just got smaller and smaller.

Finally she asked me to agree to a divorce. She said she'd met another man and fallen in love with him, a guy named Ingraham. I didn't know him, this was all news to me. It was like being blindsided, like a guy you didn't even know was behind you suddenly cold-cocks the shit out of you. I raised hell, said I'd fight it, not that that would have done any good. Then she hushed about it. I guess Ingraham was having problems getting loose too.

Then it got really strange. Everything was waiting. We weren't talking. We moved through the house try-ing to stay out of each other's way. Like we were hold-ing our breaths not to use up each other's air. We were still sleeping together but it was like the bed was a land-mine, if you moved you'd just blow everything up.

I came in one day from work and she was just gone. Vanished. All her things were still there, her clothes, her jewelry, the things she put a value on.

Time went on, maybe a month. Then one night I woke up for some reason and got up and looked out the bedroom window and there were lights all in that field we came across. Red lights, blue lights, all flickering like the world's biggest car wreck had happened right back in these woods. I came back here to see what was going on.

There were cop cars, ambulances. Coonhunters had stumbled across two bodies and called 911 on their cell phones, if you can believe coonhunters with cell phones. They were just bringing the bodies out of the woods, or what they could find of them. Wild dogs or coyotes had been at them and they sort of had to gather them up.

Jesus Christ, she said.

Wait. It gets better. Once they were identified the sheriff was convinced I'd done it. Just caught them playing house and shotgunned them and let them lay. I was up against it. I couldn't turn around without a cop car driving up in my yard. They were watching me, following me wherever I went. They questioned me half a dozen times. I was scared shitless. They could put me away for life, electrocute me, lethal inject me right out of this world.

Just about the time the ink was drying on the warrant Ingraham's wife came clean. Ingraham had mailed her a letter and she'd been sitting on it for a month. Turns out Ingrahm had asked for a divorce too, but he had three kids and that wasn't going to happen without a hell of a court fight. He'd have lost everything, kids included. The letter said he and Sarah had made a suicide pact. He was going to off her and then himself. So they did, in I don't know what order. Apparently Ingraham had been wired up with some of his connections crossed. He'd tried suicide before, and this time he got it right. I guess that was her revenge. She knew they were lying out there in the woods with bugs crawling on them and wild dogs pulling them apart.

Rideout's second cigarette burned his fingers and he looked at it in surprise as if he'd forgotten it was there and he dropped it into the frozen leaves.

Or maybe, she said.

Or maybe what?

Maybe Ingraham did write the note and send it to her but then he changed his mind. Wised up and wasn't going to use it. Maybe she kept the note and did it herself.

Rideout shook his head. He rose and brushed off the knees of his jeans. The woods were enormously still and very cold and he wanted quit of them.

I told you the story, he said.

You told me a story with too many possible endings, she said. She was smiling at him. Maybe it happened just the way you said. Or maybe she did it. Or maybe you wrote her the letter and killed them yourself.

A winter rain began and it rained for three days. Rideout couldn't work. For two days he watched gray water string off the eaves and on the third he walked back across the field to her house. He had not planned to go but she seemed to fill some vacuum in his life he hadn't even been aware of. Rebekah was restless, the rain depressed her, she wandered about the house. More than once she called the sheriff's office and checked on Albert's confinement status.

She showed Rideout rooms he hadn't seen. Behind each door marvels, each room seemed to hold its own story, its own secret. A room where they stored the provisions they'd laid by for Y2K. They'd moved them from rented home to rented home, as if there'd be a replay or the other shoe hadn't dropped yet. First aid kits, ammunition, canned goods, dried fruit and beans. Jars of antibiotics they'd bought in Mexico. Enough penicillin to cure clap on an epidemic scale, she said. They'd planned for everything except what to do when nothing happened.

Another room was stacked nigh to the ceiling with poetry. A book of Rebekah's poems they'd vanity-published with the idea of selling it on the internet and becoming rich. He opened a copy and just saw words at random. Stillbirth, Armageddon, eucalyptus. In the spring I'll take them around to book stores and leave them on consignment, she said, but their cartons were becoming worn and tattered from being moved so often. Poor poems with their meters grown laggard and their images flyspecked and tarnished.

The Oz factor seemed very high here. She spent much of her time on the internet and she told him of conspiracies. 9-11, JFK, Diana. A black mass gathering at the edge of the known universe. The world itself seemed conspiracy enough to Rideout and he thought it pointless and wrongheaded to jerk additional ones electronically out of the ether.

Let's go riding, she said. Buy some beer and I'll show you the backroads.

Out of a falling night that he thought suited them very well and out of the sense of perplexity she was always beset with she told him about her girlhood. She came from a wealthy family in Chicago, she said. Her father owned a string of department stores. She didn't understand how she'd come to this, or even what this was.

I went to a very exclusive Catholic school, she said. I wish you'd known me when I was a little girl. In my little uniform.

Rideout drank beer and watched the road turn up solitary images for his inspection: a lone tree clustered with sodden roosting birds like bitter fruit, a nighthawk swooping up from the side of the road. I would just have corrupted you, he said.

I went away to college, she told him. I studied philosophy at Washington University in St. Louis. Ludwig Wittgenstein. I became obsessed with this Austrian philosopher, Wittgenstein. He's all I thought about. I even dreamed about him at night. When I was fifteen or so I'd read that book by Nabokov and it struck me I should have been Wittgenstein's Lolita, if the times hadn't been so out of joint I would have, too. Later I let this professor, this Wittgenstein scholar, seduce me. But he just fucked me and tried to control and ruin my life and he wasn't anything like Wittgenstein anyway.

What's going to happen when Albert gets out of jail, he asked her.

I don't know how I wound up with Albert, she said. I don't know how I wound up with me.

He wondered about the future and he pressed his hand against the window like a scryer at his crystal but the falling dark just rolled up enigmatic symbols he couldn't interpret: a house site where all the house there was was a chimney rising out of a charred landscape, a tent abandoned in a windy field. Abandoned by God knew who. An evangelist who'd passed one too many collection plates, miracled one too many paraplegics back onto the road. A carnival struck by freaks and gypsies who'd left for warmer climes. He imagined nighthawks hung like aerialists in the tent's upper reaches, winter foxes denned in its darker corners.

In these foreshortened December days dusk came early. Night came rolling out of the violet trees like dark waters from a levee breached and unseen and swept across the field toward them.

His thumb traced the fading cerise and mauve outline of her bruises. The side of her face, the ribcage below her left breast. All the light there was in her bedroom was a candle she'd lit and in its glow the bruises had taken on the shapes of conjectural countries, old lost continents you shouldn't ever go to.

She rose naked from the bed and took up their wine glasses from the nightstand. With the dim light behind her and her red hair unbraided all down her back she looked like a fairytale princess a few years past happily ever after who'd rethought her position and gone over to the dark side. Silhouetted so her breasts looked tipped with anthracite, the shaven divot of her copper pubic hair with the suggested orifice below it seemed to make some exclamatory point.

She returned with the wine and crawled into bed with him. This is my last story, she told him. It's a short one but it's one of those parables with a point to it. A moral. See if you can figure out what it is when I've finished.

I was half a set of identical twins. My sister Merle had married and moved away to Key West. A lot of bad things happened to her. She had a baby and it died while it was little and she had a breakdown. A complete emotional meltdown. Then her husband divorced her after the little girl died.

She was being treated by this psychiatrist who fell in love with her. That's not supposed to happen, but it did. And she fell too, it was one of those obsessive things that you know can't end in any good way.

And this one didn't. Merle slit her wrists in the bathtub and bled to death. We had her put in a crypt there in Key West. Then her crypt was broken into and her body disappeared.

When the authorities found it it was in this doctor's house. He'd stolen it and he was living with it, you know, living as man and wife. He was preserving it as best he could with cosmetics and chemicals and he'd made a sort of new vagina, out of rubber or plastic or something and he was still having sex with her.

Goddamn, Rideout said.

He felt her shrug against him. The truth is just the truth, she said. He didn't want to give up the body. He fought the police until they overpowered him, they had to shoot him with one of those stun guns. Daddy shipped her body back to Illinois and had it buried there. But that's not the point. Do you see the point?

For the life of him Rideout didn't. He didn't say anything. He didn't believe there was a point.

The point is that's what I want, she said. Somebody who loves you so much they just won't ever quit on you. Absolutely no ambivalence. That will say fuck the grave and refuse to let you go and if you do they reach into the dark after you and pull you back into the light. That's what I want.

When she rose and blew out the candle the room smelled like cinnamon. He lay in the scented darkness and thought about what was going to happen. They'd told their stories like cards laid face-up in some curious game but each tale was slanted to the teller and in the end they were just smudged reams of foolscap that revealed nothing. He thought of Rebekah in her little girl uniform, Wittgenstein stepping out of the shadowed trees with his pockets full of candy. He thought of Albert in his jail cell, what was he doing? Summing up the day past in a journal he kept, pecking a cored dime into a jailhouse ring, biding his time waiting for bail or trial. Or perhaps he'd chipped a mansize hole in the concrete and wriggled his shoulders into it and was worming his way toward them. That could be his step on the porch, his fist at the locked door.

He suddenly realized that anything could happen, that the future was volatile as nitroglycerin, ephemeral as smoke shifting in a glass beaker.

For how could they know? Who could know? Who could have foretold that Albert would be deader than the pharaohs, his cedar casket borne by six good men and true through the nightshade and down the slope to land's end and cast upon the waters of the river Styx, rocked on the waters like a miniature covered barge, a redneck Charon at the tiller, the other shore already warping up out of the water like a darkly kept promise, a charred and skeletal yellow landscape layered in impasto that was drawing ever nearer.

Much grieved by his mother. She flew into Ackerman's Field from Arizona. Prostrate with grief she threw herself across the casket. She would call him back from the dead but he would not heed her. Silence

rolled on her wave on wave. So she had him buried with
artifacts from his life that perhaps symbolized him and
further might aid or comfort him where he was going.
She buried him with his 30-30 Winchester and a sixpack of Budweiser, an unopened can clasped in his left
hand, the right with its skinned knuckles holding the
rifle at a loose parade rest.

Late in the day she halted the pickup in his yard.
She didn't get out and she didn't cut the ignition switch.
She rolled down the glass and her face looked harried,
frightened, he couldn't tell which.

Albert's out or getting out, she said. Some of
his deer hunting buddies got together and put up
the money.

Rideout thought he was going to say, then pack
a bag or grab a change of clothing, a shirt, a dress,
and we'll be gone. Just get the hell gone, pick the last
place he'd think of and go there. But his throat
seemed to constrict so tightly it precluded speech and
he didn't say anything at all. He stared across the truck
to the cold still woods that were already bluelooking
with dusk.

He won't come for a while, she said. He'll celebrate
with his buddies at the City Café till it closes and then
he won't have anywhere to go but home. So he'll come

home and kick the holy shit out of me and in the morning he'll go deer hunting.

Hellfire, Rebekah. He's under bond. If he lays a hand on you he'll be back in jail, with more charges on his ass.

She'd started shaking her head at the first word and she continued shaking it. When he gets in a rage he can't think ten seconds into the future, she said. He doesn't give a shit about probation or court or judges. He'll just do it.

All right. I'll go over there and wait with you. Maybe we could both talk sense to him.

This sounded ridiculous to Rideout even before the words were out of his mouth and he wished he'd just kept his mouth shut.

I guess you had to say that. But I've got to tell him alone, I've got to tell him he has to give me a divorce. Maybe if I drop all the charges he'll just divorce me and let me be.

He thought of the things men and women do to each other and wondered what Albert and Rebekah had done to each other for things to come to such a pass. One too many bottles of Wild Turkey, one too many cartons of vanity-published poems. One too many helpful neighbors who live just across the field. He wondered what he had done to Sarah to make her take that first slow walk into the dappled summer trees.

I've got to go, she said. I'll call or come over here if I can.

After she'd gone he looked for a weapon. He didn't believe in guns anymore and he sorted through his tool-box. He hefted a claw hammer in an experimental way but settled on a lug wrench with a wicked looking head on it. He'd never hit anyone with either tool but if worse came to worst he guessed he could beat Albert off Rebekah with it.

Halfway across the field it began to snow. First just a few drifting flakes and then harder, he could hear it hissing in the sagegrass. He turned back toward his house, the shifting curtain of snow swinging toward him, the house and pine grove vanishing in billowing white.

He was wearing an old wool overcoat and a watch-cap and he turned up the collar of the coat and rolled the cap down over his ears. He walked slowly and let darkness and the snow take the world for he wanted the watch he kept to be covert. He didn't want Rebekah to know he was there unless it became absolutely neces-sary. And devoutly hoped it wouldn't.

He crossed the fence below the house and came up through blackberry briars past wan statuary arranged about the slope like stragglers late for some arcane show. There was a woodshed below the corner of the porch and he waited behind it, crouching there with the wrench in his fist, watching the leaves fill up with snow, each its little grailed cup of ice.

He wondered what she was doing. The house was dark save a yellowed square from the living room window. Writing a poem, cooking Albert a warm meal, deciding what to say. He envisioned her crouched before an opened cedar chest, sorting through her masks to see what might work. Impatience, outrage, a weary resignation.

After a long time he began to wonder if Albert would even come. He might have gassed up his truck and headed for the state line. Rideout wondered how long he should prudently wait. It was very cold and he was already thinking of the warm fireplace, a pot of hot coffee. What was more likely was that they'd make up. Have a hot meal and go to bed and make love while he crouched out here like a fool to the tenth power with a lug wrench in his hand.

Finally he began to sustain himself by thinking about his dog. Minding its own business. Trotting across the field, probably on his way to visit some girl dog. A rose in its teeth perhaps. Then there's a red hot explosion in his belly and blood slung all over the grass and finally an explanatory crack from the high powered rifle comes rolling across the field.

Lights flared drunkenly in the treetops before he even heard the truck. It was drawing nearer, muffled by the snow, struggling up the driveway. He stayed out of sight. The truck halted in the yard, the engine died, a door slammed. Rideout could hear Albert crossing the yard, going up the wooden steps. He stood up with the wrench in his hand. Gutshoot my dog, you son of a bitch, he thought.

Albert didn't even make it to the front door. Halfway across the porch he stopped and kicked his left boot against the floor hard to dislodge the impacted ice and he had his right boot raised when the door sprang open and yellow light spilled out. There was an immediate and enormous concussion from the explosion and then the other barrel hard on its heels and the windows flared and died with momentary fire and Albert was catapulted backward with arms upflung as if in the onslaught of some terrible wind that was carrying him off. He struck the floor half down the steps he'd just climbed.

She came out cautiously and peered down at Albert, shading her eyes, the gun clutched across her stomach. Against the yellow light she looked like sinister and depthless statuary welded up from scraps of angled iron.

Rideout didn't even think. He was already easing down the hillside before Albert struck the floor. He went past the appalled plaster face of a Madonna and increased his pace to a run. He ran full tilt into the invisible barbed wire fence and reeled backward and fell and struggled up and ran into the field. He was halfway across it when he had to stop to catch his breath, leaning hands on knees, sucking snowflakes into his lungs, the lug wrench still clasped in his right hand.

After a time he heard the truck cranking and turning in the yards. Lights yawed in the falling snow then the truck started down the driveway. He knew with a terrible inevitability that she would drive out to the main road and turn left and when she got to his driveway, left again. He stood and watched, trying to think no thoughts at all. Think of clean things, cold things, think of snow. Think of snow falling and falling until it covers all this and the world is nothing but windformed ice.

In a few minutes he could see the headlights winding up the hill toward his house, evoking momentary trees out of the night and then dissolving them in blackness. He knew with a clairvoyant's certainty that there was one last tale to tell. He was coming to kill you and we were fighting over the gun, Jesus, I don't know what happened. Perhaps she'd need him to drag the body into the house, into the sanctity of unwritten law. He saw the two of them arranging the crime scene, should this go here or here? Scrubbing down the porch, laying a gun or club in the outstretched hand, adjusting it with a critical eye.

That's what I want, she had said. Somebody who can't let you go, who will just reach into the dark and pull you back into the light.

He didn't know if he was capable of pulling anyone back into the light and he didn't know what he was going to do but he knew he was going to have to do something. Ambivalence did not seem to be an option.

Leaning into the wind he went on toward the house. The wind was whistling across the barren field stiff and knife edged with cold and so low to the ground it seemed to be snowing upward out of the frozen earth itself.

The Iceman

Birds called him awake where he slept on the riverbank, a veritable madhouse of caws and chirps and
twittering that began with the advent of day and
increased with the encroaching light. He struggled
against waking as if the day held more than he could
handle and he wanted no part of it but he'd fallen asleep
in some curious aviary walled only by the trees and
when the cries grew more strident and persistent he dis-
carded his strange dreams and sat looking out across
the river. There was no commerce on it as yet and the
surface was calm, warped and wonkylooking as dis-
tressed sheet metal. Far across in distant haze the other
shore looked new and unspoiled. There was no trace of

man or his works and the countryside looked like the shore of some vague and lovely world only rumored, not yet tainted by civilization.

He arose and made ready to go, glancing about once like a man checking out of a hotel room checking to see has he forgotten anything. He had not. There was nothing to take into the day save Yates and the clothes on his back. He struck out up the riverbank. Curious little town built on hills. Winding precipitous side-streets, you seemed always to be climbing or descending stairsteps. He came upon the main drag where folk were beginning to mill purposefully about then veered south through a warren of shacks clinging to hillsides with parched looking nighvertical gardens attendant with nothing he recognized and through backyards strung with clotheslines where hung ragged graylooking clothes and through front yards past silent watchdogs on tangled chains. No one seemed up save some old grandmother warming in the sun and did not acknowledge his existence, he seemed to move through here in furtive invisibility. Begarbed shacks halfpainted as if their tenants had given up and thrown the brushes away, blownout automobiles deceased and stripped of their viable organs, some already buried in honeysuckle and kudzu. He moved through a land locked in silence, a place that seemed to be reeling in the after-shock of some cataclysm that had come in the night and whose impact had not yet been assessed. He quickened his steps.

He came out near the railroad tracks four or five blocks up from the depot. He went past a sprawling clapboard building that had been remodeled and added onto endlessly as if constructed by carpenters who could come to no sort of agreement as to what they were building. It moved backward in a series of diminishing rooflines and the last addition seemed designed for littlefolk or leprechauns so near the ground it was. There was a red Diamond-T truck backed to the front porch and a heavyset man was loading blocks of ice onto it with a set of tongs. Another man sat leaning against a porch stanchion with his face in his hands. He seemed to be grieving. Yates had seen this truck before or one like it and he went closer to inspect it. When he turned his attention back to the seated man he saw that he was holding crushed ice in his cupped palms and he was rubbing his face with it.

The man with the tongs slammed a fifty-pound block of ice onto the bed of the truck and stepped back to the porch.

You better get to coverin this shit up, he told the seated man. I get paid to sell it and that's all and here I am loading it. But I'll be damned if I'm covering it and everything else.

The man lowered his palms and looked at the melting ice and rubbed it into his sparse gray hair. Chunks of ice lay there and began to melt and the cold water ran down his forehead. His eyes were fey looking and drunken, one with a rightward cast as if it would have a wider vision of the world or at the very least a different perspective on it.

I was tryin to remember where I stayed last night, the man said. It's right on the edge of my mind but I just can't get hold of it. I wish I could. Seems like I done somethin awful or somebody done somethin awful to me but I'll be damned if I can remember what. I wish I could just remember where I stayed.

Where was you when you woke up? Yates asked, becoming interested in this mystery in spite of himself. That always seems to help me. Generally where I wake up is about where I fell asleep at.

The man looked at him and then he looked away. He shook his head and didn't say anything.

Where was your truck at when you woke up?

The man studied Yates without expression, with a face that bore him no animosity that perhaps welcomed the rationalizations of a logical mind.

Ahh, he said. My truck. My truck was here, where I left it yesterday when the ice plant was closed. I can keep up with my truck. It's me I keep losin.

None of this is gettin ice loaded and covered up, the man with the tongs said.

Ain't I seen you on Allens Creek? Who are you?

I'm the iceman, the man said. You liable to see me most anywhere. I'm the iceman, he sang in a tuneless crooning. I'm the iceman, the iceman, better get out of my way.

Yates turned to go.

Hey, the man said. Yates stopped.

I'll give you two dollars if you'll get that scoop and sawdust the ice down. Cover it over and put the tarps over it.

Yates looked at the size of the truck. The ice stacked in its bed. The mounded pile of sawdust.

I already got two dollars, he said.

All right, I'll give you four. Hellfire, ain't you got no ambition? Here I am offerin you double, I say double your worldly goods for a few minutes work and you don't even want to hear it. What's the matter with these young folks today.

Where you takin this ice?

The iceman studied. Monday, he told himself. He looked at Yates. I'm goin out Riverside and up Allen Creek. Back through Oak Grove.

I'll do it if you throw in a ride to Allens Creek.

The man stuck out a hand and Yates shook it. The hand was wet and cold as ice, just the way an iceman's hand should be, Yates thought.

He took up the scoop and the man with the tongs showed him what to do. The blocks of ice were spaced two or three inches apart and Yates carefully filled in between them with sawdust and between the ice and the sideboards. When that was done, a layer thrown loosely over all, the man with the tongs began to stack more ice. A layer of ice, a layer of sawdust. At last the man signaled he was through and Yates covered the last layer and drew the tarp over it and lashed it down.

The iceman was up and about and with enormous effort he opened the truck door and climbed in. Yates got in the other side.

You have to hold onto that handle, the iceman said. Door'll fly open on a curve and sail your skinny ass down a hillside.

Yates sat clutching the door handle both handed. The iceman was staring out the windshield.

Well now, he said. He was looking at the world with intense concentration, as if it were coming at him at a hundred miles an hour and he was charged with negotiating its curves and byways. He reached out and turned the ignition and the truck coughed into life and set idling. He nodded. All right, all you unrefrigerated sons of bitches, he said. Here comes the iceman.

Four or five miles out of town they went through a flatlands where the road paralleled the river and Yates could see not the river itself but the upper half a barge that seemed to be cruising by some miraculous locomotion through willows and a stand of sassafras. Then the road curved upward into the hills and he could smell hot piney woods baking in the sun, astringent and somehow nostalgic.

The iceman at first drove with the exaggerated care of a drunk who doesn't quite trust himself. As his confidence grew and the pitch to the motor wound higher he began to croon mindlessly to himself, the iceman, here comes the iceman, better get out of my way.

He walled his off eye up at Yates, You ever been so drunk you couldn't remember where you was or what you done?

Lord no, Yates said, clinging religiously to the door handle. I can barely find my way through a day cold sober. I'd not even attempt one drunk.

I never could make much sense of it drunk or sober, the iceman said. Seems like it just went easier drunk though.

Yates didn't reply. The road had climbed into terrain near mountainous that he was wary of and the road was snaking around narrow switchback curves. The off eye kept glancing at Yates and Yates wished it would watch the road. The truck kept rounding curves on the blind side and Yates was watching them apprehensively. Red rock climbed sheer on the left and looking down from his window he could see the earth dropping away in a manner that took his breath away and he tightened his grip on the door handle as if in some talismanic way it was holding the truck on the road.

It's in like a dark place, the iceman said. I can almost see in there but whatever's in there slips back out of sight. Sometimes I nearly think of it and then it's gone.

Godalmighty, Yates said.

They'd rounded a leftleaning curve on the wrong side and two enormous black mules were just suddenly upon them, the left mule rearing with wild rolling eyes and its hoofs slamming onto the hood then its head turning against the actual glass with white walled eyes frantic then gone and the wagon with the old man's face a rictus of absolute horror and him trying to whip the mules onto an impossible course, sawing the lines and cutting them into the sheer wall with the wagon tilting and the iron rims sparking against the granite bluff. The truck struck the left rear wheel of the wagon and carried it away with the wagon turning and sliding crosswise behind them, Yates whirling watching through the back glass the overalled man spilled from the wagonbed then whirling back to see coming at him across the hood a frieze of rock and greenery clockwise in such elongation the landscape seemed stretched to transparency as the brakelocked truck swapped ends in the gravel and the horizon itself fleeing vertically downward as the truck tilted backward off the shoulder of the road and the truck cab filled with intense blue sky.

The iceman was humming crazily to himself. He'd locked the brakes and now when he released them the truck accelerated backward down the hill with him watching out the windshield trees that seemed to come from nowhere fleeing backward, brush that sprang erect from beneath them like imaged brush in a pop-up book, him giving the steering wheel little meaningless cuts right or left. He seemed not to know where he was.

Hit the Goddamned brakes, Yates screamed. Yates was peering out the back glass, at once trying to see where they were going and fearful of it.

When the iceman slammed the brakes the motor stalled and died and the load of ice shot backward down the slope, disappearing off the bed like a frozen waterfall then the truck lurching and jouncing across it and the ice reappearing magically before them, great chunks strewn like gleaming hailstones from a storm of unreckonable magnitude.

Cut it into a tree, Yates yelled, but before he'd even finished saying it the truck slammed into a treetrunk so hard the force of it whipped his head into the back glass then forward into the windshield. They sat in a ringing appalled silence, Yates clutching his head, the iceman staring up the hillside the way they'd come. Outraged crumpled saplings, crushed cedars, ice everywhere.

All them folks, the iceman said.

Do what? Yates asked. He thought the iceman was talking about the collision with the wagon and he'd only seen one man.

All them folks waitin on me. With their hot jugs of tea. Their ice cream freezers. Where's the iceman, they'll say. He ain't never been this late before.

Yates was shaking and he couldn't stop. You are absolutely the craziest shitass in the whole history of the world, he said.

The iceman was trying to get his door open. It seemed to be stuck, jammed where it struck the wagon wheel. At length he turned in the seat and kicked it hard bothfooted and it sprang open.

Help me, he said. We got to get that ice gathered up.

I wish I had sense like other folks, Yates said. I'd be better off in hell with my back broke than ever crawlin in a truck with you.

I got money tied up in this ice. Help me reload and we'll scotch this truck somehow and I'll try to drive us out.

Yates looked. He was shaking his head.

You couldn't drive up that bluff in a Goddamned Army tank, he said. She ever comes out of here she'll have a block and tackle tied to her.

Nevertheless it's got to be done, the iceman said. He staggered up the slope clutching to saplings. Yates clambered out of the canted truck cab. It was hard even to stand here, so precipitous and undependable was the earth. He looked down on a fairyland of treetops, tiny pink road winding somewhere, so far. He sat down and began to inspect himself for wounds.

The iceman had selected a fifty-pound block of ice. He was stumbling toward the truck with it clutched before him like some offering he was making. Suddenly he halted stockstill as if the ice had frozen him in his tracks. He had a peculiar look on his face.

Son of a bitch, he said.

What?

A dance, the iceman said. He sat the ice down carefully then seated himself upon it. Elbows on knees, hands clasped before him. He seemed to be in deep thought.

What?

I killed somebody, the iceman said.

Who? Yates was thinking about the wagon, the man sliding roadward.

Some girl, the iceman said. Some woman. We was at a dance. One of them beerjoints down by the river. I don't even remember what we got into it about. I took to hitting her with somethin...seems like it was a singletree but I don't know where in the shit I'd get a singletree.

A stick maybe. A big stick. I remember she kept tryin to crawl off into the bushes. I kept hitting her and hitting her.

Yates was watching him apprehensively. He could feel ice water tracking down his rib cage. He glanced upward to the rim of the earth where the road ran, figuring perhaps angles of inclination, speed when fleeing madmen.

Maybe you just slapped her around a little, he said hopefully.

The iceman thought about it a while. He took a package of Camel cigarettes from a shirt pocket and tipped one out and just sat holding it. His hands were wet from the ice and after a time it shredded in his fingers.

No, he finally said. He shook his head. No. I killed her all right. She was all busted up and limber. I remember rakin wet black leaves over her face.

Yates arose. He dusted off the seat of his jeans.

I got to get on, he said. It's a long way to Allens Creek.

The iceman appeared not to hear. Yates climbed a few feet up the slope and then he turned. I need to get that money, he said.

What money?

That four dollars for loading the truck.

The iceman fumbled out a wallet, sat studying its contents.

I'd double it again if you'd help me reload.

I got to get on.

The iceman carefully counted off four one dollar bills, rubbing each one carefully between thumb and forefinger. Yates took the proffered money and pocketed it.

Appreciate it, he said.

Anytime, the iceman said. You want to help me as a regular thing the job's open.

Yates didn't reply. When he was halfway up the hillside he looked down. The iceman had risen and he had begun to gather the blocks of ice and restack the truck. Yates went on. The next time he looked back the iceman raised a hand in a curiously formal gesture, farewell, and Yates raised an arm, farewell, and clambered onto the road.

He stood breathing hard. Far down the winding road toward Clifton the farmer appeared riding a mule. The wagon and the other mule were nowhere in sight.

He turned. Beyond the rim the world lay in a crazyquilt patchwork of soft pastel fields, tracts of somber woods. Folded horizons so far they trembled and veered in the heat and ultimately vanished.

Somewhere in that dreammist lay Allens Creek. He'd have traded a year of his life for a handful of its dust. He spat and wiped the sweat out of his eyes and struck out toward it.

Wm Gay
and the Art of the
Short Story

"Here's to the hearts and the hands of the men,
that come with the dust and are gone with the wind."

Bob Dylan

William Gay makes his home in Lewis County, Tennessee in a cabin overlooking Little Swan Creek. Being from the rural south William Gay is associated with the south and embodies the characteristics that exemplify southern literature. However, the literary aesthetics of his language takes him above the confines of regionalism. Many of the writers in the southern genre rely on violence to give their stories excitement. In Gay's stories the excitement is not necessarily the moments of violence, horror, suspense or outright gore. While his stories are filled with this, in fact they wax bloodier as sex, violence, and death haunt each page. But the pyrotechnics of his stories are the wonderful phrases that speak like an oracle voice set in poetic lyrical prose. The highly unorthodox way he turns a phrase or uses a metaphor is at once unusual and enlightening. He creates carefully faceted, sparkling phrases and scatters them through out his prose. As if a glimpse of pure beauty is asserted into the midst of the incredibly mundane world his characters inhabit.

This generates a negative capacity that is charged with a special intensity. The style of his writing is highly refined literary art while the content deals with characters who are the poorest of the poor often living in run down shacks lit with kerosene lamps, heated by wood stoves. These characters defy moral logic creating both revulsion at what is going on in their lives but also sympathy and identification. They are described in situations fraught with fear, suspicion and suspense written in elevated prose with passages of incredible beauty.

William Gay has lived most of his life in Lewis County. Lewis County has a population of about eleven thousand and consistently has one of the highest unemployment rates in the state. Lewis County recently lost all of the small industry that came to the rural south in search of cheap hard working non union labor. The industry has moved on to Mexico and China where the-labor costs are even cheaper. Now, ironically, the biggest employer in town is the local drug treatment provider.

Lewis County was one of the few areas outside the Mississippi Delta where share cropping was still a job opportunity in the nineteen forties and fifties. Gay grew up in a sharecroppers cabin. He remembers how the land owner had a store where all the families living on his farm would buy their groceries and supplies and it always seemed like the bill at the store was more than the salary in the pay check. He is unschooled outside the Lewis County school system, which is not known for its academic excellence.

He still lives within five miles of where he was raised on Grinder's Creek. After finishing high school he went into the navy and served on a destroyer off the Asian coast during the Viet Nam war. When his tour of duty dropped him off in New York City he stayed in the Village for a few years in the mid sixties. He eventually went back to Lewis County only to move on to Chicago looking for a better job. There he lived in an urban ghetto of people from the rural south that sprang up around Kenmore Avenue. In 1978 he moved back to Lewis County and has stayed ever since. He worked as a carpenter, hung dry wall and eventually did a lot of house painting. He also married and had four kids.

He has been reading and writing all his life and has learned his craft in near total isolation from the intellectual and academic currents of the times. Born in 1943 he had his first publication in 1998. He had a long foreground, writing since he was fifteen, occasionally getting discouraged but finding that life without writing was just not a possibility. So he would press on struggling to get his stories and novels typed and submitted. There are lost novels where the only copy was mailed off and never returned, and long years of rejection with piles of standardized rejection slips.

In the past few years he has exploded on the scene. In 1998 he received notification from the Georgia Review that they wanted to publish a short story and no sooner had they called than he learned that the Missouri Review also accepted a story. After that he went on to be published in Harpers, GQ, Atlantic, Southern Review and the Oxford American among many others. His stories have been extensively anthologized with appearances in the *New Stories from The South, The Year's Best* in 1999, 2000, and 2001; along with *Best New American Stories*, 2000; the *O'Henry Prize Stories*, 2001; *Best Mystery Stories*, 2001; *Best Music Writing*, 2001; and the *Stories from the Blue Moon Café, Anthology of Southern Writers*, 2002; *They Write Among Us:*

New Stories and Essays from the Best of Oxford Writers, 2003
and *Best of the South: The Best of the Second Decade: Selected
and Introduced by Anne Tyler*, 2005.

His story originally titled, *The Paperhanger, the
Doctor's Wife, and the Child Who Went Into the Abstract*, was
published as the first volume of the Oxford Series, by
the Book Source, in Hohenwald. It was subsequently
published with the title "The Paperhanger" in Harper's
Magazine in February, 2000 and has since been anthologized at the present count in five different collections.

An editor at The Missouri Review was associated
with a publishing house and he liked Gay's stories so
much he asked if he had a novel. He did and his first
novel, *The Long Home*, was published in 1999 by
MacMurray and Beck, a small press in Denver. It
immediately received positive reviews including the
New York Times. His agent placed his second novel
with Doubleday and he garnered rave reviews for it as
well. Both his novels have been published in England
and the second book, *Provinces of the Night*, has been
translated into German. His third book, a collect of
short stories titled, *I Hate to See that Evening Sun Go Down*,
was published by The Free Press, a division of Simon
and Schuster, in 2002. He is the winner of the 1999

William Peden Award, the 1999 James A. Michener Memorial Prize, and is a 2002 Guggenheim Fellow.

He has a life long interest in music and has written extensively about the contemporary music scene as well as the traditional roots of county and blues. His musical criticism has been published and anthologized in a variety of music reviews and he appears each year in the summer music issue of the Oxford American. As illustrated on the cover of this book he is also a painter, primarily with oils, and has developed a distinctive landscape style.

He dates his compulsion to write from the seventh grade when a teacher, noticing that he was reading Zane Grey and Earle Stanley Gardner gave him Thomas Wolfe's *Look Homeward Angel* and Faulkner's *The Sound and the Fury*. He read *Look Homeward Angel* by the light of a coal oil lamp, transfixed by Wolfe's language: it was the first time he realized that language can transport you, take you outside yourself and whatever your life is, and that the sum of arranged words can mean far more than the individual words used in this construction. He was stunned and never got over it, he immediately started writing a novel. That moment marks the beginning of his writing career. He hasn't stopped since.

J.M.WHITE

Printed in the United States
102502LV00001B/47/A

9 780976 520221